# AKHENATEN AND TUTANKHAMEN

Leaders of the Ancient World

# AKHENATEN AND TUTANKHAMEN

Zoe Lowery and

Susanna Thomas

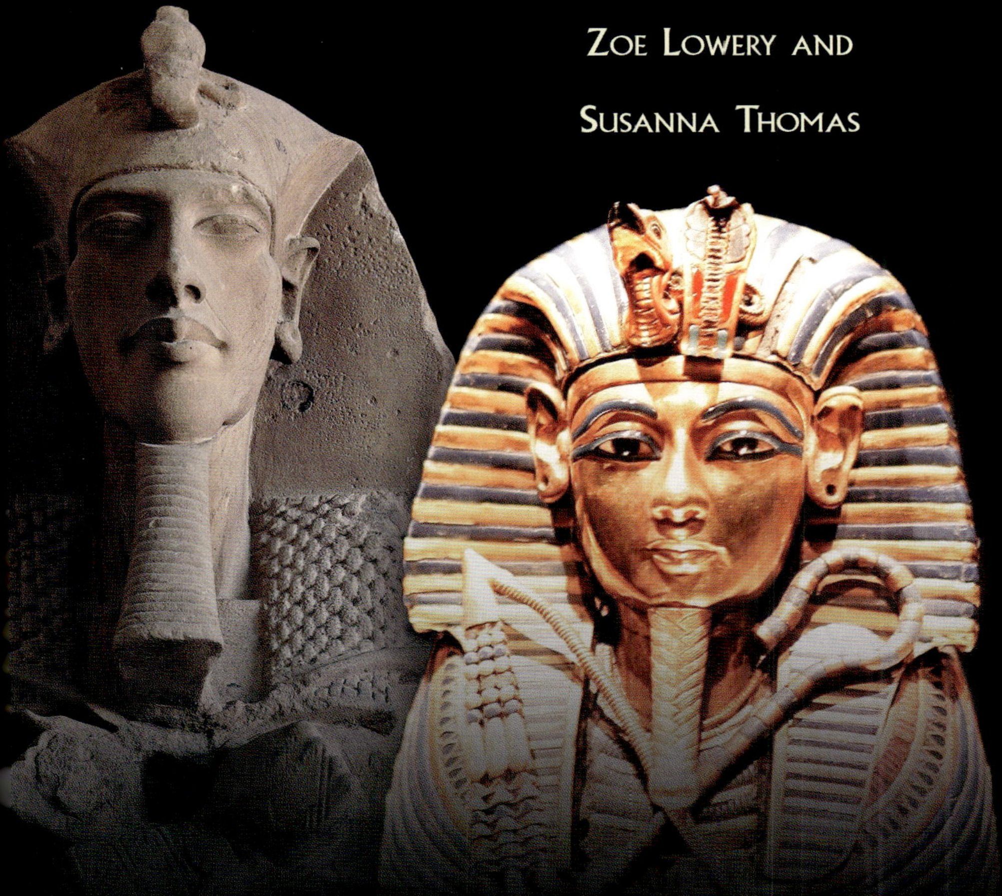

ROSEN PUBLISHING

New York

Published in 2017 by The Rosen Publishing Group, Inc.
29 East 21st Street, New York, NY 10010



First Edition



**Library of Congress Cataloging-in-Publication Data**

Names: Lowery, Zoe, author. | Thomas, Susanna, 1966- author.
Title: Akhenaten and Tutankhamen / Zoe Lowery and Susanna Thomas.
Description: New York : The Rosen Publishing Group, Inc., 2017. | Series: Leaders of the ancient world
Identifiers: LCCN 2016028499 | ISBN 9781508172604 (library bound)
Subjects: LCSH: Akhenaton, King of Egypt. | Tutankhamen, King of Egypt. | Pharaohs—Biography. | Tell el-Amarna (Egypt) | Egypt—History—Eighteenth dynasty, ca. 1570–1320 B.C.
Classification: LCC DT87.4 .L69 2017 | DDC 932/.0140922 [B] —dc23
LC record available at https://lccn.loc.gov/2016028499

*Manufactured in Malaysia*

# CONTENTS

# INTRODUCTION

The king known as Akhenaten (also spelled Akhenaton, Akhnaton, or Ikhnaton) went by many names, including Amenhotep IV, Greek Amenophis. Akhenaten was the second son of the pharaoh Amenhotep III, who ruled Egypt from 1390 to 1353 BCE. Akhenaten ruled as king of ancient Egypt from about 1353–1336 BCE, which was known as the Eighteenth Dynasty during the period later known as the New Kingdom. Akhenaten's name is best known in history for his attempts to eschew the traditional gods and instead form a new cult dedicated to the Aten, the sun's disk. He even changed his name to Akhenaten, which translates to mean "beneficial to Aten." In short, Akhenaten was the leader of a twenty-year religious rebellion against the gods and religion Egypt had worshipped for more than two thousand years.

This new cult was considered mandatory for all ancient Egyptians, and Akhenaten created a royal capital with all kinds of art dedicated to Aten. Most ancient Egyptians were not in favor of this change, however, so Akhenaten's endeavors eventually failed. Although the pharaoh made all kinds of modifications and modernizations to

The pharaoh was so enthusiastic about the god Aten (also spelled Aton) that he changed his name from Amenhotep IV to "beneficial to Aten."

buildings, statues, and inscriptions, later rulers changed or destroyed them soon after Akhenaten's death. The great city of Akhetaten was abandoned, even though it had only been established for twenty years. Still, some of the artistic advances that came about as a result of his cult continued to be used by later artists and craftspeople.

After Akhenaten's death, the next significant, though short-lived, ruler was Tutankhamen (also known as Tutankhamun, Tutankhamon, Tutankhaten, and King Tut), whose name means "Living Image of the Aten." The "boy king" Tutankhamen ruled ancient Egypt from 1333–1323 BCE, a reign more commonly identified with his impressively lavish tomb, KV 62 (tomb 62), which was found by Howard Carter in 1922 in the areas known as the Valley of the Kings, than for any political triumphs. Although the tomb Carter discovered was a major archaeological find, it provided precious little insight into the brief life of this ancient Egyptian ruler. Akhenaten and one of his wives, Kita, may have been his parents, but to this day his parentage is the source of debate among scholars.

During Tutankhamen's rule, however, he and his advisers reestablished the traditional art and religion of ancient Egypt, which Akhenaten had worked to fervently to abolish. And just two years after taking the throne, he changed his name from Tutankhaten to Tutankhamun, or heqa-iunu-shema, which translates to mean "Living Image of Amun, Ruler of Upper Egyptian Heliopolis." Tutankhamen went right to work on having the destroyed and damaged temples, images, and other items related to the old religions repaired, for example.

CHAPTER 1

# THE DAZZLING SUN

Akhenaten's father, Amenhotep III, was the eldest surviving son of the pharaoh Thutmose IV, and he was between ten and twelve years old when his father died in 1390 BCE. Thutmose IV left behind a stable and successful country. Egypt's borders were secure, and her empire stretched from Nubia in the south to Syria in the north. Thutmose IV is also famous for cleaning and restoring the great Sphinx at Giza. He was so proud of this act that he left a large inscription at the site, known as the Dream Stele.

Amenhotep III was a splendid ruler. His royal court was famous throughout the ancient Near East as a center of luxury and grandeur. A high standard of art and architecture was achieved in temples and other buildings constructed during his reign. Trade and international relations spanned all the

Amenhotep III was only ten or twelve years old when he took the throne, but he matured into a famous ruler.

Some of Amenhotep's legacy lies in architecture, such as the Karnak Temple. He dedicated this temple to the god Amen-Re.

countries of the region, including Greece and the Aegean Sea, Cyprus, Turkey, Syria, and Canaan. Amenhotep III was certainly aware of his own importance, and by the end of his reign he actually described himself as "the Dazzling Sun."

## BUILDING UP A COUNTRY

Amenhotep III ruled a country that was mostly at peace, thanks to the efforts of his ancestors who had successfully fought many military campaigns. During the first two years of his reign, Amenhotep opened new quarries at Tura near Memphis (modern-day Cairo) to supply stone for many building projects. The royal scribes wrote, "His majesty commanded to open the quarry chambers anew, in order to

The gold-and-silver-finished statues, which are now known as Colossi of Memnon, are memorials to Amenhotep III. Their remains still stand today.

quarry fine limestone." He and his favorite architect, who was called Amenhotep, son of Haipu, planned and erected many additions to the Karnak and Luxor Temples in Thebes. These were two of the most important temples constructed in the New Kingdom and were dedicated to the god Amen-Re. Also erected during this time was Amenhotep's enormous memorial temple on the valley floor of the west bank of the Nile River at Thebes and a large tomb near the Valley of the Kings. Amenhotep III's memorial temple is famous today as the site of two enormous statues of the king that stood at the entrance of the temple. The statues are now called the Colossi of Memnon. Amenhotep III was extremely proud of his buildings, and he left an inscription saying "His Majesty's heart was pleased with making very many great monuments, the like of which never existed before." The buildings were decorated with the finest and most expensive gold and silver finishes.

## WIVES, SONS, AND DAUGHTERS

By the second year of his reign, 1389 BCE, Amenhotep III was already married to his favorite wife, who was called Tiye. Tiye was the daughter of a

# THE AMARNA LETTERS

One of the main pieces of evidence we have relating to international relations during the reigns of Amenhotep III and Akhenaten is a group of documents called the Amarna Letters. These come from an ancient records office called "Place of the Letters of Pharaoh," and they were discovered in 1887 by a village woman who was digging for fertilizer. The letters consist of a group of oblong clay tablets covered in cuneiform writing that was made by pushing a wedge-shaped pen into the soft clay. Most of the tablets are written in Akkadian, which was the international diplomatic language of the times. The Amarna Letters consist of more than 330 tablets sent to and from Amenhotep III and later his son, Akhenaten, and the other rulers of the area, including the kings of Babylon and Assyria and the smaller kingdoms in Canaan and Syria that lived under Egyptian rule. The Amarna Letters are an important group of historical records from the Late Bronze Age, and they tell us a great deal that we wouldn't otherwise know about the political situation, trade, and royal marriages at this time. They also tell of exciting new inventions such as glass and the spread of the use of the important metal iron.

The Amarna Letters are a group of more than three hundred tablets that offer a glimpse into ancient Egypt's politics, royalty, inventions, and Late Bronze Age.

man called Yuya and his wife Tuya who came from Akhmim, 100 miles (161 kilometers) north of Thebes. Although not actually part of the royal family, Yuya and Tuya were both important government and religious officials.

King Amenophis III married Tiye, who would later give birth to Akhenaten and was an important government figure in Egypt.

More is known about Tiye than most other royal women because Amenhotep III included her in many of his monuments and inscriptions. The pharaohs had been quite careful not to let royal women become too important after the reign of female pharaoh Hatshepsut. This was because they didn't want any other woman to try and take over the country. Tiye, however, was often represented equal in size to her husband (indicating almost equal importance). She was also sometimes shown wearing the outfits of female gods, and there is also a statue of her as a sphinx, which was a mythical creature usually made up of the body of a lion and the head of a human. This sort of statue was something that was usually only used to represent the features of the king. Evidence from the Amarna Letters indicates that she also wrote to other kings and queens as an equal.

Tiye obviously played an important role in the government of Egypt, and in many ways Amenhotep III indicated to his people that Egypt was ruled by a king *and* a queen. Tiye was given many royal titles by her husband, and these reflect how important she was to him. It is not known exactly why Amenhotep III chose to place such public emphasis on his wife in this way. One possibility was to make the pharaoh and his family seem more like the gods of Egypt, who were often thought of as part of a couple, or as a family with one child. Many such triads were worshipped, including the important god Osiris, his wife Isis, and their son Horus; Ptah, his wife Sekhmet, and their son Nefertem; and Amen, his wife Mut, and their son Khonsu. Another possible reason was that Amenhotep was strongly under the influence of his powerful parents-in-law Yuya and Tuya, and they may well have thought that it was in the interest of their daughter Tiye to be promoted in this way.

However much Amenhotep III may have loved Tiye, it did not stop him from having many other wives as well. He is known to have married two Syrian princesses, two princesses from Mitanni (eastern Turkey), two princesses from Babylonia (Iraq), and a princess from Arzawa (western Turkey). Amenhotep III also had a large harem full of Egyptian women at his service. Some of these women had been provided by provincial governors ruling in Canaan and Syria. There is evidence for this in one of the Amarna Letters that Amenhotep III wrote to Milkilu, the ruler of Gazru (Gezer) province. "This from the king. He herewith sends to you Hanya, the overseer of archers, along with every thing for the acquisition of beautiful female cupbearers...Send extremely beautiful cupbearers in whom there is no defect."

Amenhotep III and Tiye had two sons called Thutmose and Amenhotep (later renamed Akhenaten) and four daughters called Sitamun, Henuttaneb, Isis, and Nebetah. Thutmose was the eldest son and heir to the throne. When he was about sixteen years old, he was sent to Memphis to learn how to become a high priest of the god Ptah. We know that Thutmose was fond of his pet cat, because there still exists the miniature stone sarcophagus that he had prepared for its burial.

The eldest daughter Sitamun gained the title God's Great Wife like her mother and may have actually married her father (as opposed to just standing in for religious and ceremonial festivals). Sitamun had a daughter with Amenhotep III called Baketaten. Although this custom of marrying one's own children may seem strange to us today, there are reasons why it did not seem strange to the Egyptians. There were various advantages for the pharaoh in marrying women of the royal family. Children born from these marriages would be doubly royal and so would have the strongest claim to the throne. The practice also got rid of the problem of Egyptian princesses whose husbands might try to claim the Egyptian throne. Actually finding husbands for the king's daughters during the New Kingdom could sometimes be difficult. Egyptian princesses were not allowed to marry foreigners, and as Amenhotep III told the king of Babylonia, "From time immemorial no daughter of the King of Egypt has been given to anyone." Another reason that the royal family practiced marriage like this was to show that they were like the gods of Egypt, among whom incestuous relations were quite common. However, it is not clear in this case why Amenhotep III would need to marry his own daughter, as he already had many wives and many heirs to the throne.

Thutmose died in 1361 BCE when still in his early twenties. This was a serious blow to Amenhotep III and Tiye. Their second son, also called Amenhotep, now became the heir to the throne. Almost nothing is known about Amenhotep before this point, except that he was born around 1373 BCE, and like his elder brother he may have been sent for priestly training, this time to the temple of the sun god Ra at Heliopolis.

## CELEBRATIONS AND STATUES

In 1361 BCE and again in 1357 BCE, Amenhotep III celebrated two *Heb Sed*, or jubilee, festivals. These included special magic rituals that were performed to renew the king's powers. Such festivals were national celebrations enjoyed by everyone. Traditionally the first Heb Sed festival was celebrated in the thirtieth year of a pharaoh's reign and then again every three years after that. To host the events, a new palace town was built at Malkata, which is south of the memorial temples on the west at Thebes.

Amenhotep III decided to use his first jubilee to associate himself strongly with the sun and the sun god Ra. He devised a new way of writing his *prenomen*, or throne name, "Nebmaatre," which showed the king holding a *Maat* feather with the sun disk on his head. He also began the construction of new buildings in the temples at Thebes and elsewhere that are known as solar courts. These consist of open areas full of altars where people could make offerings to the sun, as opposed to the more traditional type of temples, the centers of which were enclosed and unseen by ordinary people.

Amenhotep III was so smitten with the god Aten that he named his palace in Malkata after him. He went on to describe himself as the god, too.

Sun gods such as Ra could be represented by a picture of the sun, while the sun itself actually represented another god called Aten. Earlier in the Eighteenth Dynasty, Aten had been depicted either as a hawk-headed god or as a winged sun disk with outstretched arms. Ra was the invisible source of energy for the sun, while Atum was the first creator god who existed before anything else. Atum was father of the gods Shu, who was air, and Tefnut, who was moisture. Their two children were Geb, the earth, and Nut, the sky. Geb and Nut were in turn the parents of four more gods, and this group of nine made up something called the Great Ennead of Heliopolis.

All of these religious ideas probably originally arose from the fact that the sun could be seen rising each day and traveling across the sky, before disappearing each night only to reappear the next morning. The sun was therefore seen as both incredibly strong and powerful, as well as something that had always been and would always exist. Consequently, the pharaohs, as absolute rulers of their country, wanted to be seen in a similar way. During the Old Kingdom, one of the religious roles of the dead pharaoh was to rise up into the sky and merge with the sun god Ra, which is why the next pharaoh was always known as the son of Ra. By the Middle and New Kingdoms, religious ideas had been somewhat democratized. Ordinary people could also have exciting afterlives, and prayers to the rising and setting sun were carved onto people's tombs.

Amenhotep III was particularly interested in the god Aten, as demonstrated when, for example, he called his new palace at Malkata "the Radiance of Aten." However, these religious ideas were taken further when Amenhotep III actually began to describe himself *as* Aten and so promoted the idea that he himself was like a god. There was a growing emphasis on "the cult of the king," where images, especially statues, of the king seem to have been worshipped by the people. Most ordinary people were not allowed into temples except on special occasions, and their main contacts with state gods were when statues of them were carried through the streets during religious festivals.

The other important statues available to ordinary people were the colossal statues of kings set up at the entrances to many temples. Traditionally, people prayed in front of these statues in the hope that the king would send their messages to the gods. Cults also grew up around these statues, with people praying in front of them and bringing offerings of food and drink because they began to think of the statues themselves as actual gods. Amenhotep III was well aware of this practice, and we know of more than one thousand statues of him still existing today. There are also paintings in which Amenhotep III makes offerings to a statue of himself, and there is a statue *of a statue* of the king originally erected in Luxor Temple with an inscription describing the king as "dazzling Aten for all lands."

## THE LAST DAYS OF AMENHOTEP III

Amenhotep III suffered from a serious illness in his final years on the throne, and his remaining son Amenhotep was made coregent, probably to lessen some of the burden of leadership from the elderly and ailing pharaoh. It was known abroad that Amenhotep III was unwell, and Tushratta, the king of Mitanni, sent him a statue of the healing goddess Ishtar to help his recovery. Amenhotep also ordered the carving of 750 statues of the lion goddess Sekhmet that were then placed in Luxor Temple. Sekhmet was a fierce warrior goddess who was also able to cure diseases, and these statues were carved with prayers for the protection of the king.

Despite all his efforts, the age of fifty found Amenhotep III obese and with little hair and poor teeth. He probably died in 1353 BCE in his new palace at Malkata. His tomb was ready with rooms to bury Amenhotep III as well as Tiye and one or more of his other wives. He died well before them, however, so he was buried alone while they were laid to rest elsewhere. Located in the modern-day area called the West Valley off the Valley of the Kings, the tomb's walls depicted scenes of Amenhotep III and various gods, as well as with images from the *Amduat* (*What Is in the Underworld*), a selection of writings.

CHAPTER 2

# PHARAOH AKHENATEN

The other rulers around the eastern Mediterranean were quickly told of the death of Amenhotep III. Many of them wrote to Amenhotep IV and his mother, Tiye, expressing their sorrow at the news and their wishes that good relations would continue under the new ruler. King Tushratta of Mitanni was apparently particularly upset. "When my brother Nimmureya (Amenhotep III) went to his fate it was reported. When I heard what was reported, nothing was allowed to be cooked in a pot. On that day I myself wept, on that day I took neither food nor water." Tushratta obviously hoped that good relations between the two countries would continue. "But when they said Napkureya (Amenhotep IV), the eldest son of Nimmureya and Tiye, his principal wife, is exercising the kingship in his place, then I spoke as

Amenhotep IV, later known as Akhenaten.

follows 'Napkureya, his eldest son, now exercises the kingship in his place. Nothing whatsoever is going to be changed from the way it was before.'"

## IT'S ALL IN THE NAME

Amenhotep IV, who would later change his name to Akhenaten, came to the throne in 1353 BCE. An important part of Amenhotep IV's coronation was the selection of his royal names. These were used by the pharaohs as symbols to reinforce their claims to the throne. New Kingdom pharaohs usually chose names that emphasized the pharaoh as warrior and protector of Egypt. They also chose names that showed that the pharaoh was particularly close to the god Amen.

Amenhotep IV chose instead to emphasize his connections with the city of Thebes and the major state temple at Karnak. We do not know why he chose to concentrate so strongly on his position at the city of Thebes. It certainly indicates that he intended to devote a large part of his time to this city and perhaps suggests that other, more traditional roles of the pharaoh concerning the government of Egypt and its empire were of less interest to him.

## DISSATISFACTION

Before long, however, Tushratta was writing letters of complaint to Egypt, saying that Amenhotep IV had not kept his side of various bargains. "My brother has not sent the gold statues that your father was going to send. You have sent plated ones of wood. Nor have you sent me the goods that your father was going to send me, but you have reduced them greatly." Another ruler who was quickly irritated by Amenhotep's attitude was the king of the Hittites, called Suppiluliumas. He wrote to Amenhotep IV asking, "Why, my brother, have you held back the presents that your father made to me when he was alive?" The situation later became more serious, with Suppiluliumas even questioning whether Amenhotep IV was trying to break off relations between the two countries. "As to the tablet [letter] that you sent me, why did you put your name over my name? And who now is the one who upsets the good relations between us, and is such conduct the accepted practice? My brother, did you write with peace in mind?"

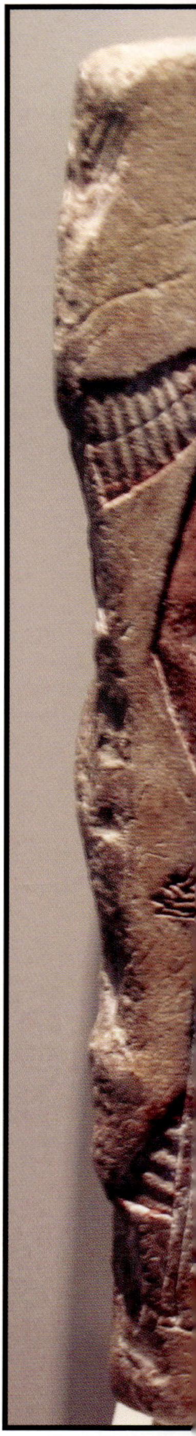

Pharaoh Akhenaten and his Great Royal Wife Nefertiti are shown in a relief held by the Egyptian Museum in Berlin, Germany.

## THE ROYAL COUPLE

Amenhotep IV is shown accompanied by his mother, Queen Tiye, in most of the inscriptions and paintings from this period. However, it is clear that by the time he came to the throne he was already married to the woman who appears to have been the great love of his life and who had a big influence on his future actions. She was called Nefertiti, which means "the beautiful one is come." It is not known who Nefertiti's parents were, but it is possible that she was the daughter of Queen Tiye's brother Ay and his wife. This would have meant that Nefertiti was Amenhotep's first cousin. Either before he became pharaoh or right at the beginning of his reign, Amenhotep IV and Nefertiti had a daughter called Meretaten (meaning Aten's beloved). They would probably have preferred a son first in order to ensure that there was an heir to the throne, but nonetheless Meretaten was obviously loved by both her parents. Paintings of her found at Karnak are often labeled "the king's bodily daughter whom he loves, Meretaten, born of the great king's wife Nefertiti."

## ENTER ATEN

Amenhotep IV had demonstrated through the choice of his royal names that he was interested in the city of Thebes, and in particular the great Amen Temple at Karnak. His first project at this site was to decorate a large pylon gateway that had been begun during the reign of his father Amenhotep III. The carvings here show traditional themes, such as the pharaoh hitting foreign prisoners over the head with a large mace, or worshipping the sun god Re-Horakhti. However, some new features were added to these reliefs, including a picture of the sun disk Aten with rays extending out around it, and the name of Aten was written as if the god, like the pharaoh, had great royal titles, which had never happened to a god before. Aten was now called "Re-Horakhti, who rejoices in the horizon in his name Shu, who is Aten." By the third year of Amenhotep's reign, the god Aten's name was actually written in cartouches as though it was part of a royal title.

These carvings are the first indication we have that Amenhotep IV was essentially inventing a new god. The god Aten had been gaining in popularity during the reign of Amenhotep III. He had grown out of the various forms of traditional Egyptian ideas of a sun god. However, where previous gods such as Re-Horakhti had lived in temples and were usually depicted as men with the head of a falcon wearing a sun in their crowns, the god Aten was shown not as a person but as the circle of the sun alone. Amenhotep IV now said that the god Aten was a self-created god who renewed himself every day. He also said that Aten could not be represented by a human form and that only the idea of Aten could be represented by the symbol of the sun disk.

## "ATEN IS FOUND"

Amenhotep IV also started work on the construction of a completely new temple to the god Aten at the site of the Karnak Temple. This was to be called Gempaaten, which means "Aten Is Found." A mission was sent to the sandstone quarries at Gebel Silsila, which were about forty miles north of Aswan. There a large stele, or stone tablet, was cut into the wall of the quarry to commemorate the event. "The first occasion that his Person [Amenhotep IV] laid a charge on the king's scribe, the general Amen…to carry out all the works projects…and on the leaders of the army to perform a great forced-labor-duty of quarrying sandstone, in order to fashion the great benben of 'Horakhti, Light which is in Aten.'"

Gempaaten was built to the north of the great Amen Temple at Karnak. Unfortunately, this, along with at least three other temples built at the site by Amenhotep IV, were completely demolished by later pharaohs. In fact, almost all the buildings, statues, and inscriptions dating from the first five years of Amenhotep's reign were systematically destroyed soon afterward. This means that it is difficult to reconstruct exactly what happened during this period. However, many of the stone blocks used to make these buildings were reused in later temples, and for the last 150 years Egyptologists have been working to try to put some of the buildings back together, and to look at the pictures and read the inscriptions from this period.

The Gempaaten Temple was probably based on other existing temples to sun gods such as Ra. The emphasis of this temple was on large spaces open to the sky, which were filled with small altars. Offerings of food and drink were placed on these altars every day. The temple was made up of a large,

The Talatat wall is a part of Amenhotep IV's temple at Karnak. It shows scenes of the king and worship.

walled, rectangular courtyard that was itself surrounded by a mud brick wall. The corridor in between the two walls contained a walkway lined with square columns, each fronted by colossal statues of the king. These statues were once brightly painted and showed the king wearing either the crown of Upper and Lower Egypt or a headcloth with two plumes on top like representations of the god Shu. The figure of the king in all these statues was wearing a fine pleated linen kilt, which fastened at the front below his navel. These are the earliest known sculptures of the new pharaoh and they demonstrate a new and different artistic style.

## SHOCKING STATUES

The Gempaaten statues of Amenhotep IV are famous throughout

the world today for their extraordinary appearance. Both his face and his body are shown in an exaggerated and almost grotesque way. He has a receding forehead, a very long and narrow face, slanting eyes, hollow cheeks, and thick, bulging lips. His body is shown with a rounded chest, a narrow waist, huge bulging thighs, and spindly lower legs. Egyptologist Erik Hornung suggests that these images were "a manneristic distortion of reality, a rebellion against the classical idea of beauty." Some people today think that these statues are really beautiful in an interesting way, while others have described them as "sick ugliness" and "perverted reality." Various diseases have been suggested as the cause for such an odd appearance of the king, including Froehlich's syndrome or Marfan's syndrome, but we do not know for certain the reason for this new style.

However, there are good reasons to believe that Amenhotep IV didn't actually look like these statues. He may have wanted to send a certain message to people through such an odd appearance. There are statues dating from later periods in his reign where he looks quite normal. Some features, such as his weird long skull, were copied in stat-

In many Gempaaten statues, the image of Akhenaten IV shows embellished features, such as large lips and a long narrow face.

# CONSTRUCTING GEMPAATEN

The Gempaaten Temple was probably built in 1352 BCE. We know this because it only includes pictures of Amenhotep's eldest daughter, Meretaten, suggesting that his other children hadn't been born yet. The temple was made in a new way out of small stone blocks measuring 52 by 26 by 24 centimeters (about 20 by 10 by 9 inches) and called *talatat*. Such blocks were probably used because temples could be built much more quickly with them than before. Talatat could be carved out of quarries very efficiently and quickly and could be carried by just one person. Temple walls were built with the blocks, laid both vertically and horizontally. All the cracks were then filled in with plaster. The walls were then covered with a thick layer of whitewash, and scenes were then lightly carved into them (a method called sunken relief). These were then painted with lots of bright colors.

utes and paintings of other people as well. This is shown, for example, in the tomb of Ramose, who was vizier (prime minister) for both Amenhotep III and Amenhotep IV. Some parts of Ramose's tomb were painted during the reign of Amenhotep III, and in these Ramose looks normal. The rest of his tomb was finished during the reign of Amenhotep IV, and in these paintings Ramose suddenly looks rather distorted in a similar manner to the Gempaaten statues.

The most likely explanation for his appearance is that Amenhotep IV was trying to present himself more like the gods, and the Gempaaten statues probably show the king as the gods Atum and Shu. It is also possible that he wished to be seen as a sort of combined male/female figure. It is interesting to note that Amenhotep IV was probably personally involved in the development of this new style. His chief sculptor was a man called Bak, who was the son of Amenhotep III's chief sculptor, Men. An inscription in a granite quarry at Aswan shows Bak and Men, where Bak describes himself as "a disciple whom his Person [Amenhotep IV] himself instructed, chief of sculptors in the big and important monuments of the king."

## RUDMENU, TENIMENU, AND OTHER TEMPLES

Two more temples called the Rudmenu, meaning "Enduring in Monuments," and the Tenimenu, meaning "Exalted in Monuments," were both quickly finished by 1351 BCE. Scenes from the Rudmenu Temple include pictures of the king and his court visiting open-air temples in chariots. These temples contain tall altars or offering tables that were piled high with food and drink. There are also paintings of rows of servants carrying baskets of food and crying, "Oh Neferkheperure, you beautiful child of the sundisk, may the sun-disk favor you." Many scenes show that Amenhotep IV and his family were surrounded by armed troops, including Egyptian armed guards, policemen with wooden clubs, and Libyan, Syrian, and Nubian mercenaries every time they left their palaces. We have no way of knowing if this actually happened, but if true, it is an interesting glimpse into the realities of daily life for the new pharaoh. The Tenimenu Temple contained a number of paintings of domestic rooms and activities such as baking bread and storing wine, and it is possible that this temple was connected to a royal palace at the site. At the beginning of his reign Amenhotep IV and his growing family had lived at the Malkata Palace in western Thebes, and they then moved to live at Karnak once building work had been completed.

In 1350 BCE, the fourth year of Amenhotep's reign, another temple called Hutbenben, meaning "Mansion of the Benben Stone," was built next to the Gempaaten. The Benben stone was an object sacred to the god Ra at Heliopolis and may have developed from early religious ideas of a creation mound rising out of primeval waters. This temple seems to have been built strictly for Nefertiti's sole use. Here the queen was shown carrying out various duties usually reserved for the king, including smiting enemies and making offerings to *Maat*. This temple was also decorated with illustrations and colossal statues of Nefertiti looking oddly similar to her husband, probably representing the goddess Tefnut. Their eldest daughter, Meretaten, is also shown dressed in a long adult gown and shaking a rattle, helping her mother with the religious ceremonies, and a second baby daughter called Meketaten, meaning "She Whom Aten Protects," also appears in some of the scenes. Nefertiti had by this time added to her name, and she was now called Nefernefruaten-Nefertiti, with Nefernefruaten meaning "Perfect One of Aten's Perfection." Temples to Aten were also built at other sites in Egypt, including Heliopolis and Memphis, but there is almost no evidence of them left today.

## AN EARLY JUBILEE

For some reason unknown to us today, Amenhotep IV decided to celebrate his first Heb Sed, or jubilee, festival in his third year of rule, 1351 BCE, which was twenty-seven years earlier than he was supposed to. Pictures of all the celebrations were carved onto the walls of the Gempaaten, and it is possible that he had already decided on this celebration when the temple was first commissioned. Apart from being rather early, the rituals in Amenhotep's first Heb Sed also differed in other ways from those that traditionally took place. Most noticeably, instead of offering to all the gods of Egypt, Amenhotep IV celebrated with the god Aten alone.

This Heb Sed festival seems to have marked a change in the way that the god Aten was represented. The god's name was now shown in two cartouches, as if Aten was a king. Amenhotep IV also chose at this time to state that the god Aten and the dead pharaoh Amenhotep III were one and the same so that in effect each dead pharaoh became the god Aten. Therefore the cult of Aten was the same as the cult of kingship, and worshipping the god Aten was like worshipping the dead pharaoh. If his father had become the god Aten, then Amenhotep IV was obviously the son of the god Aten. As such, he was also the best person to be in charge of communicating with and worshipping Aten. Consequently, Amenhotep IV now became the high priest and "Chief of Seers" of the new god.

Because he was now the high priest, Amenhotep IV decided that he ought to change his royal names. After 1349 BCE, he went by the names Son of Ra Akhenaten, which translates to "He Who Is Effective on Aten's behalf, the God and Ruler of Akhetaten," among other new monikers.

CHAPTER 3

# THE NEW CITY OF AKHENATEN

Apparently the introduction of a new god was insufficient for Amenhotep IV (now known as Akhenaten), because after four years of reign he also established a new capital city. His plan was to desert the religious capital at Thebes as well as the administrative capital at Memphis. Akhenaten may have been so truly consumed by religious zeal that he felt compelled to create a completely original city built afresh for his new god. Not everyone was necessarily thrilled with this plan. Priests who worked in the Amen cult at Thebes and the Ptah cult at Memphis were displeased by the idea of a new god, so they may have been unsupportive of this plan.

Akhenaten said that the god Aten had chosen a site for the new capital for him. This was a large, windswept plain, seven miles long and about three miles wide, on the east bank of the Nile in a deserted area of Middle Egypt, approximately 200 miles (322 kilometers) south of Memphis and 250 miles (402 kilometers) north of Thebes. The plain is surrounded by steep cliffs on all sides, and from a distance a notch in the cliffs looks a bit like the hieroglyphic sign for horizon, which may have influenced Akhenaten's decision. The city was called Akhetaten, which means "the horizon of Aten." The site is known today as el-Amarna.

Akhenaten planned to move to his new city in his fifth year of rule, but there were more changes planned before he left Thebes. A speech he gave earlier in his reign had been inscribed on the pylon gateway at Karnak Temple:

> Look, I am speaking that I might inform you concerning the forms of the gods. I know their temples and I understand their writings, namely the list of their primeval bodies, and I have perceived them as they cease, one after the other, even those consisting of any sort of precious stone…except for the god who made himself from himself.

In modern times, most of the world's religions have been monotheistic—that is, they propagate the idea that only one, all-powerful god exists. It is not clear that this is what Akhenaten meant by his statement. His new religion may have been henotheistic, meaning that it may have called for the worship of a new, most-powerful god without denying the existence of other gods. In any case, it was a sufficiently revolutionary view to cause problems. This attack on all the other gods of Egypt must have made most of the priests both unhappy and frightened of what the pharaoh was planning. After all, many thousands of men and women were employed in temples throughout Egypt, and most of them would have had families who depended on income from the temples, both

View from the North Palace where Akhenaten and Queen Nefertiti lived in the city also known as Akhetaten, which is known today as el-Amarna.

in the form of cash payments and leftover offerings of food and drink.

## BANISHED

Akhenaten now decided that the god Amen was to be banished from the land, even though before this Amen had been the most important god during the New Kingdom. Huge gangs of workmen were sent to temples all over the country. Every single inscription of the name Amenhotep IV was covered in plaster and recarved to hide the Amen part. Once Akhenaten had moved to Akhetaten these workmen were then told to go even further and to cut out or cover up every single inscription of the name Amen and his wife, the goddess Mut. This was a huge task, as it involved thousands of inscriptions on temple walls, obelisks, shrines, tombs, and statues. Many statues of Amen and other gods were seized from temple sanctuaries and smashed. The gangs of workmen were almost certainly accompanied by groups of Syrian and Nubian soldiers, like those shown in the illustrations on the Rudmenu Temple, just in case priests or temple workers objected. This persecution must have been terrifying for the Egyptian people, especially in areas far away from the capital, where they would have had little idea of the momentous religious changes that had been going on. People were now afraid of being caught in possession of the name of Amen, and there is evidence today of small personal items, such as pots and scarabs, where the owners have carefully scratched out Amen's name. By 1348 BCE, even Akhenaten's new temples at Karnak were abandoned, and all the income from the estates and farms of the Amen temples was diverted to fund the construction of the new city.

## THE NEW CITY

On the thirteenth day of the eighth month of his fifth year of rule, Akhenaten, his family, and his loyal followers landed at the site of the new city. They all disembarked from the boats that had carried them down river from Thebes. Akhenaten then climbed into his golden chariot and set out at the head of a grand procession toward a platform on which a single altar had been set up in the middle of the desert plain. From here Akhenaten delivered a grand speech to his followers that explained how the god Aten had told him where to go. "Now it is Aten, my father, who advised me concerning it, namely Akhetaten. No official had ever advised me concerning it, nor had any people in the entire land ever advised me concerning it, to tell me a plan for making Akhetaten in this distant place. It was Aten, my father, who advised me." Akhenaten then listed all the temples that he was planning to build in his new city:

> At Akhetaten in this place shall I make the House of Aten for Aten my father. At Akhetaten in this place shall I make the Mansion of Aten for Aten, my father. At Akhetaten in this place shall I make the sunshade of the King's chief wife Nefernefruaten-Nefertiti for Aten, my father. In the island of Aten, whose jubilees are distinguished at Akhetaten in this place, shall I make the House of Rejoicing in Akhetaten for Aten, my father.

Akhenaten then explained the more practical aspects of the project, including who was going to pay for it. "At Akhetaten in this place shall I make

The family of Akhenaten and his primary wife Nefertiti, as shown on a relief in the Temple of the Sun.

all the taxes that are in the entire land belong to Aten, my father. At Akhetaten in this place shall I make for myself the residence of the pharaoh. Life! Prosperity! Health!" Akhenaten was firm in his commitment to the new city, as evidenced by his comment, "Let a tomb be made for me in the east mountain of Akhetaten and let my burial be made in it…Let the burial of the king's Chief Wife Nefertiti be made in it…and let the burial of the king's daughter Meretaten be made in it for millions of years. If I should die in any town of the downstream, the south, the west, or the east, let me be brought back so that I may be buried in Akhetaten." This demonstrates another break in tradition, because all previous New Kingdom pharaohs had been buried on the west bank at Thebes.

Akhenaten then ordered that two stele be set up marking the northern and southern limits of the city. Each stele would be inscribed with the text of his founding speech. These are still legible today. Work began straight away on the construction of the city. The whole settlement was built along a large, new north-south avenue that today is known as the Royal Road. The first buildings put up were the temples and so to begin with the royal family

## AKHENATEN'S FINAL RESTING PLACE

Originally, Akhenaten had planned to have his body buried in the Valley of the Kings on the west bank at Thebes. Between his increasing dissatisfaction with the city as well as the local priesthood, he changed the site of his tomb to Akhetaten. Although he had already had his sizable granite sarcophagus built at Thebes, he had it transported to Akhetaten by way of the river. He selected a site that was deep in the eastern cliffs around the city on the plain below. His tomb was positioned behind the obvious indentation in the horizon so that it was aligned with the rising sun. Work on his tomb commenced in 1548 BCE, and the bulk of the new city had been completed by the end of 1546 BCE, allowing Akhenaten and his growing family to move there permanently.

had to camp in tents. The new temples were built out of limestone blocks cut from the surrounding hillside, as well as bricks made out of mud taken from the riverbanks and dried in the sun. The

Pictured is one of the two stele ordered by Akhenaten, which mark the borders of the city on the southern and northern ends.

builders were probably a combined force of Egyptian soldiers and laborers brought from other sites in Egypt, along with foreign prisoners of war.

Akhenaten returned to the site exactly one year later to see how the work was progressing. We do not know where he and his family were living while the new city was being built, but they probably didn't spend much time at Akhetaten during this period. It would have been hot, dusty, and very noisy as thousands of workers labored to create a whole city out of nothing. The whole place was one enormous building site spreading in a line for more than 7 miles (about 11 kilometers). For this next visit Akhenaten stayed in a tent made of rushes cut from the river. He took another trip around the perimeter of the city and decided that twelve more boundary stele were needed, as well as a replacement for the first southern marker that had already deteriorated rather badly. These new stele were carved out of the hillside and were flanked with statues of the king and queen and the two princesses Meretaten and Meketaten.

CHAPTER 4

# FAMILY OF THE PHARAOH

Early in his reign, Akhenaten and Nefertiti continued to increase the size of their family. Meretaten and Meketaten were two daughters who were likely born before the family made the move to Akhetaten. After six or seven years of reign, a third daughter joined the family. Her name was Ankhesenpaaten, which translates to "May She Live for Aten." A fourth daughter was probably added to the family around 1346 BCE. Her name was Nefernefruaten Tasherit. Tasherit translates to "junior" or "the younger," after her mother.

Yet another daughter was born in 1345 BCE, and she was called Nefernefrure, meaning "Perfect One of the Sun's Perfection." Their sixth and final daughter was probably born in Akhenaten's tenth or eleventh year of rule, and she was called Setepenre, which means "She Who the Sun Has Chosen."

Akhenaten and Nefertiti were depicted in a more casual way than ever before in Egyptian art.

The city of Akhetaten was filled with paintings showing the royal family together. Many of these images show Akhenaten, Nefertiti, and some or all of their children relaxing under the sun disk with rays reaching down to the family, sometimes with small hands on the ends of the rays holding the *ankh*, the symbol of life, under their noses. The princesses are usually shown playing around their parents or being cuddled by the king and queen, and Akhenaten and Nefertiti are also sometimes shown hugging each other. Images of such informal behavior had never been shown in Egyptian art before.

# AKHENATEN'S MANY WIVES

Although much less visible in the archaeological record, Akhenaten, like most Egyptian pharaohs, had many wives and mistresses. He is known to have married at least one foreign princess called Tadukhepa, who was the daughter of King Tushratta of Mitanni. She was sent to Egypt during the last years of the reign of Akhenaten's father, Amenhotep III, but she seems to have married Akhenaten instead. Later letters from the Mitannian king send greetings such as "Tadu khepa, my daughter, your wife." We know practically nothing about her life in Egypt, and she disappears from the Amarna Letters after the fourth year of Akhenaten's reign.

There is some evidence from inscriptions at Akhetaten about another wife who was named Kiya. A special temple was built for her called the Maruaten. This also meant that she was given land

Many images of Akhenaten and Nefertiti contained symbols that referred to their religious ideas and featured the god Aten in some way.

# MORE THAN MEETS THE EYE

Images of the royal family were not simple scenes showing a happy family. They actually contained important religious messages. Ancient Egyptian religious concepts were often built around the idea of groups of three gods. Now, the god Aten, Akhenaten, and Nefertiti were being shown in a similar way. Aten was identified with the creature god Atum, while Akhenaten was Shu and Nefertiti was Tefnut. Such identifications had already been attempted in the earlier statues of the king and queen at Thebes. The royal family now dominated much of everyday life in the new city. They drove up and down the Royal Road almost every day in great processions of chariots accompanied by squads of armed bodyguards running at either side. The family often appeared together in the Window of Appearance. Even when the ordinary citizens of Akhetaten went home there was no escape. Almost every private house contained a shrine or altar displaying either a sculpture or a stele showing the royal family. Private homes had traditionally contained small shrines to household gods such as Bes, who was thought of as the protector of the family, or Taweret who was associated with women and childbirth. Archaeological excavations at el-Amarna have shown that many people secretly kept small images of these familiar gods, but officially everyone was now meant to look to the royal family alone for spiritual guidance and protection.

Most homes had a special place for a shrine to household gods, such as Taweret, who was the god of women and childbirth.

This ancient Egyptian jar may feature one of Akhenaten's wives, Kiya, who bore the pharaoh at least three children.

and income to support herself and her temple. Kiya sometimes appears in scenes with Akhenaten, but never with Nefertiti, and it is likely that these two women were jealous of each other's influence over the pharaoh. We cannot be sure how many children Kiya had, but it is possible that she and Akhenaten had at least one daughter and two sons together.

Most images of Kiya show her with a lovely, smiling face: Her eyes are shaped like almonds, she has a tiny nose, and her chin is long. She is often depicted wearing big circular earrings and a short Nubian wig. After 1344 BCE, Kiya no longer appears in art, perhaps because many paintings and statues showing her were either smashed to pieces or Princesses Meretaten and Ankhesenpaaten took them over and reused them.

CHAPTER 5

# AKHETATEN: THE OFFICIAL CAPITAL CITY

As of 1345 BCE, Akhetaten became the official capital city. Numerous labels on wine jar labels from this time suggest that elaborate festivities commemorated the event.

## ISLAND OF ATEN DISTINGUISHED OF JUBILEES

Much building work had been concentrated around the center of the road in an area called the "Island of Aten distinguished of Jubilees," which is known today as the Central City. The streets and buildings of Akhetaten were laid out in a grid pattern, and the central city became the administrative heart of the metropolis where the government officials worked. The chief of police, called Mahu, was stationed there, along with offices such as the library and the "Place of the Letters of Pharaoh." There was also a building called the "House of Rejoicing in Akhetaten," now known as the Great Palace, where Akhenaten would have conducted state business. This building contained many brightly painted courtyards and colossal statues of the king. This was where Akhenaten held meetings with his officials and with foreign ambassadors.

Akhenaten's obsession with the new god Aten was by now so great that he chose to conduct his business outside in the open courtyards, where he could see the sun. In a hot country like Egypt, all such meetings would normally take place indoors, or at least in the shade. Now everyone was made to stand outside in the blazing sun all day long.

When the new king of Assyria, Ashuruballit, wanted to open diplomatic ties with the Egyptian throne he sent a delegation to see Akhenaten in person. These poor ambassadors had a hot and uncomfortable time at Akhetaten, and they bitterly complained to their own king once they got home. Ashuruballit wrote to Akhenaten asking, "Why were my messengers made to stay constantly out in the sun and so die in the sun? If staying out in the sun means profit for the king, then let the messenger stay out and let him die right there in the sun,

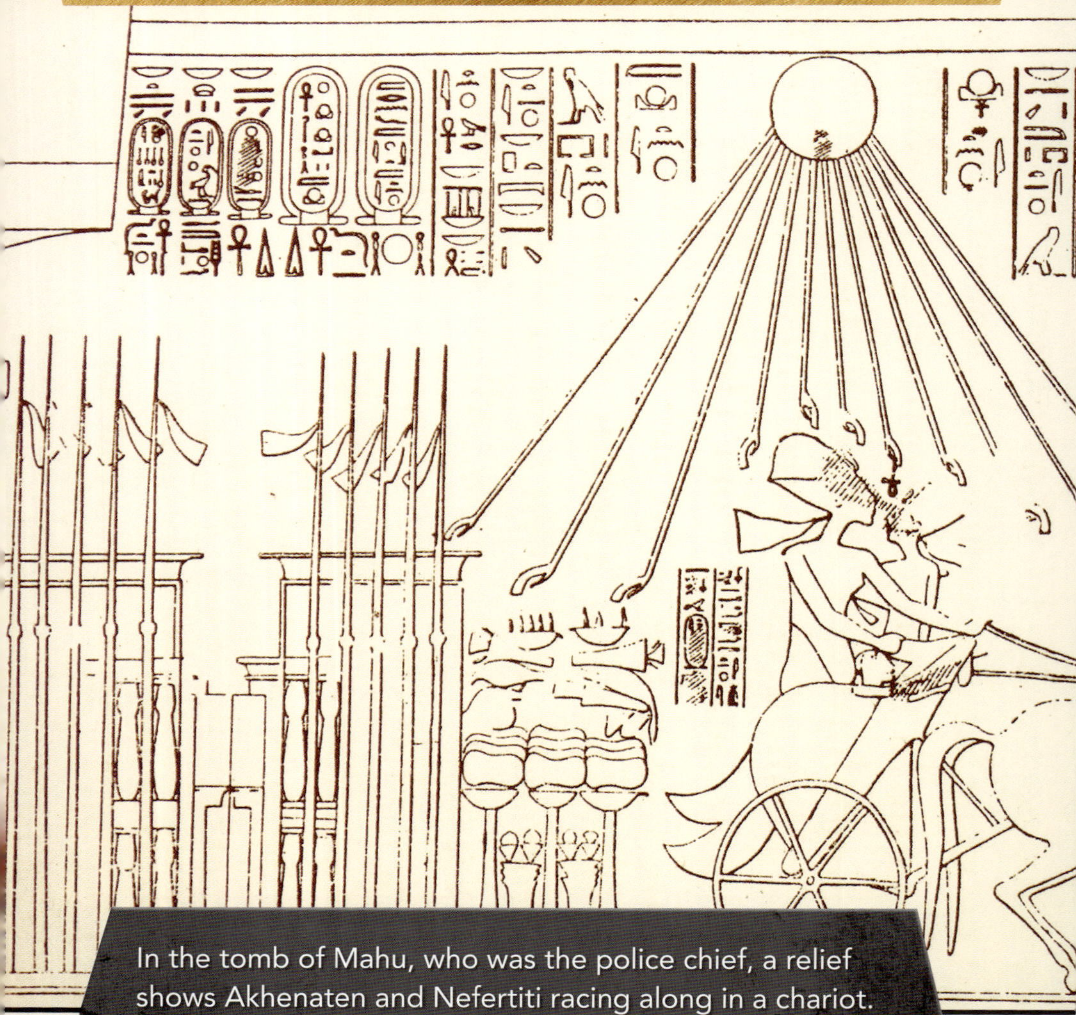

In the tomb of Mahu, who was the police chief, a relief shows Akhenaten and Nefertiti racing along in a chariot. The Mahu and a bodyguard run ahead.

but for the king himself there must be profit. But really, why should they die in the open sun?"

A bridge over the Royal Road connected this palace to the King's House. We don't know if

Akhenaten and his family ever lived in this building, but we do know that it was probably the site where the Window of Appearance, which is sometimes shown in tomb paintings, was located. The Window of Appearance was a kind of balcony from

# ACTIVE AKHETATEN

Akhetaten must have been an exciting place to live. The total population has been estimated at between twenty thousand and fifty thousand people. Pristine new temples, houses, and roads were surrounded by lots of newly planted trees and flowers. Foreign traders and their families came from the Aegean Sea and the Near East to live in the city. Civil servants and other officials from Thebes and Memphis were constant visitors to the royal court. Harbors along the edge of the city were full of warehouses, shops, and market stalls, and the air would have been filled with the shouts of merchants and traders advertising their wares and the tempting smells from bakeries and food kiosks. Beautiful glass and brightly colored pottery, textiles, and basketware were on sale, and sculptors were hard at work producing images of the royal family. Endless supplies of food and drink were shipped to the new temples from all over Egypt, and many people were able to enjoy these after they had been offered to Aten.

which Akhenaten and Nefertiti would appear and reward their loyal followers with gold collars, which were the ancient Egyptian version of today's military medals. The Window of Appearance also acted as the place where the people living in Akhetaten could see and worship their king and his family.

The Central City also contained the biggest temple at Akhetaten, originally called the House of Aten, now called the Great Aten Temple. This temple was the center of the Aten cult. It was nearly 2,400 feet (about 732 meters) long and 750 feet (about 229 meters) wide. Most of the temple consisted of a wall surrounding a vast open courtyard that contained rows and rows of altars. There were 365 altars for Upper Egypt and another 365 for Lower Egypt. Priests put offerings of food and drink on these altars daily so that the god Aten—and his priests—would not go hungry. There were also many small statues of Akhenaten and Nefertiti holding a flat offering tray. All statues were apparently pointing toward the east, which was the direction of the rising sun and the location of Akhenaten's tomb.

Another smaller temple in the Central City was called the Mansion of the Aten, now known as the Small Aten Temple. This was located on the

Partially preserved columns of the Mansion of the Aten, now called the Small Aten Temple, which was built on the Nile's west bank.

west bank of the Nile and dedicated to the cult of each New Kingdom pharaoh.

## AREAS AROUND CENTRAL CITY

At the northern end of the Royal Road is an area now called the North City. This contained another business district with large warehouses and storerooms. South of this was the Northern Suburb containing large, luxurious villas that were the homes of some important priests and government officials. A large building known today as the North Riverside Palace was once decorated with scenes of the royal family, and it is thought that this is probably where Akhenaten lived. Yet another grand building, now called the North Palace, was decorated with beautiful wall paintings showing marshes and birds and fishes. These paintings often had brightly colored and patterned borders, and the ceilings were painted with images of vine leaves and bunches of grapes. This palace was probably the home of either Nefertiti or Kiya and their children.

To the south of the Central City was another area now known as the South Suburb. This was home to many of the most important officials at

This sculpture of Nefertiti was created by the chief royal sculptor, Thutmose, who also lived in the South Suburb.

Akhetaten, including two priests called Panehsy and Pawah, the vizier, Nakht, the chief royal sculptor, Thutmose, and a general called Ramose. These people lived in large, airy villas surrounded by beautiful gardens. These were large, square buildings with entrance halls, reception rooms, large central living rooms containing a fireplace, private rooms, bedrooms, and bathrooms with showers and toilets. Pictures of such houses on tomb walls show that many of them had upper floors as well, which probably contained more sitting rooms and bedrooms. Their gardens were planted with many trees and flowers, and most contained ornamental ponds full of fish and water lilies. Kitchens and servants' quarters were placed away from the main house, as were granaries, storerooms, workshops, stables, and wells. Each villa was surrounded by a high wall to ensure privacy. Smaller houses for poorer craftsmen, laborers, servants, and shopkeepers soon sprung up between these large estates. Most houses were either whitewashed or brightly decorated, and floors were plastered or tiled.

On the eastern edge of the desert plain, a small settlement was built to house the craftsmen who were working on the tombs in the cliff side of the king and the nobles. Terraced rows of

This relief depicts a cross section of an ancient Egyptian house with stone workers and other craftsmen hard at work.

small houses were built inside a surrounding wall, although the village soon expanded beyond this barrier. We do not know where ordinary citizens were buried. There are also two groups of tombs

for officials known as the Northern and Southern Tombs. The Northern Tombs were intended for Akhenaten's closest advisers and friends, while the Southern Tombs were built for officials in charge of running the government.

CHAPTER 6

# EXIT AKHENATEN, ENTER TUTANKHAMEN

Soon after marking his ninth year ruling, all images of the god Amen in Egypt's temples were destroyed on Akhenaten's order. He also declared that Aten's name should be changed again. Aten was now known as "Living Ra, Ruler of the Horizon, Rejoicing in the Horizon in His Name Ra, the Father, Who Has Come as Aten," instead of being written in two cartouches as "Re-Horakhti, Who Rejoices in the Horizon in His Name Shu, Who Is Aten."

## RELIGION OVER POLITICS

Conversely, Akhenaten seems to have been uninterested in foreign affairs, choosing instead to concentrate on the development of his new religious ideas. Many paintings of soldiers from the city of

Akhetaten show that he was not a pacifist by any means, but he seems to have been more concerned with protecting his own person than with protecting the interests of Egypt abroad. The exception to this was Nubia, from where Egypt obtained most of her gold. Akhenaten was fully aware of the importance of maintaining the supply of this precious metal. A temple to the god Aten was constructed at Kawa, probably in 1342 BCE. Akhenaten ordered the Egyptian official in charge of the area to mount a campaign against some of the troublesome local tribes. The pharaoh "was in Akhetaten when one came to tell him that the enemies of the foreign country Ikyata were plotting rebellion and had even invaded the land of the Nile Nubians, while taking all sustenance away from them. Then his Person told the King's son of Kush and overseer of the southern countries to assemble an army in order to defeat the enemies . . . males as well as females. These enemies were found on the eastern side of the river . . . and the fugitives were smitten." After this victory, Thutmose, the King's son of Kush, apparently said to the king, "Fear of you is in their hearts. The chiefs have fallen to your might. Your battle cries are like a fiery flame chasing every foreign country."

This relief from Akhenaten's tomb shows soldiers, but his main concern was most likely protecting himself.

Akhenaten was less successful in his dealings with Egypt's territories and allies in Canaan and Syria. He annoyed Tushratta, the king of Mitanni, and failed to see that Suppiluliumas and the Hittite empire were growing powerful enough to threaten Egypt's northern provinces. Many of the rulers of the small city-states along the eastern Mediterranean coast, including Rib-Hadda, the mayor of Byblos; Abdikhepre, the mayor of Jerusalem; and Abi-Milki, the mayor of Tyre, had been educated in the court of Amenhotep III and were loyal to Egypt. Other rulers, however, took advantage of Akhenaten's lack of interest in their affairs to try to win more land for themselves. Abdi Ashirta and his son Aziru were rulers of a small state in northern Syria called Amurru, and they began to harass their neighbors. Rib-Hadda wrote increasingly desperate letters to Akhenaten, saying, "Know that the war of Abdi Ashirta against me is severe, and he has taken my cities…I am like a bird in a trap." Later he wrote, "You know that, though informed, you have delayed coming out… Now you are going to come to an empty house, everything is gone, I am utterly ruined!" Akhenaten's eventual reply was to complain "You are the one that writes to me more than all the other mayors." Another loyal mayor, called Shuwardata, was equally badly treated, writing, "Be informed, O king, my lord, that all the lands of the king, my lord, have been taken away. I am all alone."

## ACCOLADES FOR AMBASSADORS

The high point of Akhenaten's life at Akhetaten occurred in 1342 BCE, when the city hosted a massive reception for ambassadors from Syria, Canaan, the Hittite empire (Turkey), Cyprus, Libya, and Nubia.

This relief depicts ancient Egyptian ambassadors from Akhenaten's reign. Many ambassadors came to his city for a reception in 1342 BCE.

Paintings from the tombs of two important officials, Huya and Meryre II, illustrate the scene. A large, roofed platform had been set up in the desert to the east of the Central City. Akhenaten, Nefertiti, their six daughters, Akhenaten's mother, queen Tiye, who may have visited the city specially for the event, and many of their followers were transported to the site in ornate carrying-chairs slung on poles and hoisted high on the shoulders of servants. The king and queen are pictured sitting on two thrones holding hands, while their daughters are lined up behind. Rows of foreign visitors are then shown being introduced by Egyptian officials. Each one brings exotic gifts for the pharaoh, including weapons, horses, chariots, gold and silver, incense, slave girls, cattle, exotic woods, and ostrich feathers and eggs. These scenes are the last time we see the happy royal family together, as the next few years of Akhenaten's life were to prove more and more difficult.

## A TIRESOME PHARAOH

Akhenaten was not a successful pharaoh. He seems to

have argued with many of his father's closest religious and government advisers and to have ignored his responsibilities to Egypt's empire in the east. He tried to turn his dead father Amenhotep III and himself into the only gods of Egypt, and he acted in a totalitarian and intolerant manner toward the people of Egypt. Egyptologist Donald Redford concludes his study of Akhenaten by saying, "I cannot conceive a more tiresome regime under which to be fated to live." Akhenaten does, however, seem to have been a talented artist with an interest in a new, expressive style of sculpture and painting and he had a talent for writing. This is most evident in the "Great Hymn to Aten," some of which is quoted below, and which was almost certainly written by the pharaoh himself.

> Beautifully you appear from the horizon
> of heaven, O living Aten who initiates life,
> For you are risen from the eastern horizon
> and have filled every land with your beauty,
> For you are fair, great, dazzling, and high
> over every land, And your rays enclose the
> lands to the limit of all you have made, For
> you are Ra, having reached their limit and
> subdued them for your beloved son, For
> although you are far away, your rays are
> upon the earth and you are perceived.

## DEADLY DISASTERS

During this period a deadly plague swept across Cyprus, Mitanni, and Syria. The king of Cyprus wrote to Akhenaten that "the hand of Nergal is now in my country; he has slain all the men of my country, and there is not a single copper worker left." We do not know if this plague reached Egypt, but it is certain that from 1342 BCE onward, members of Akhenaten's family were dying around him.

The tomb of Akhenaten being prepared in the eastern hills of the city was intended to be the burial place of Akhenaten, his wife Nefertiti, and his mother, Tiye. Sadly his second daughter Meketaten died in his twelfth year of rule, and an extra group of rooms were carved out of his tomb for her burial. Scenes on the walls of these rooms show her corpse laid out on a bed in the royal palace. She is surrounded by weeping mourners, including her parents, who are shown crying and throwing their arms over their heads. A painting of a nurse holding a baby outside the room may indicate that Meketaten died in childbirth. Soon afterward Akhenaten's mother, Tiye, and his other wife Kiya also died.

The three youngest daughters of Akhenaten and Nefertiti, Nefernefruaten Tasherit, Neferneferure, and Setepenre, also disappear from the archaeological record at this time, which probably indicates that they all died. We do not know where they were buried.

Akhenaten's eldest daughter, Meretaten, now replaced Kiya in his affections. She became known as "Mistress of his House" and "King's Chief Wife," and she was also given the temple and lands that had previously belonged to Kiya. Meretaten's name was engraved on top of those of Kiya, and the hairstyle in some of Kiya's paintings was changed to look like the young princess instead. Akhenaten had another daughter toward the end of his reign called Meretaten Tasherit, and she may have been the child of this father-daughter marriage. Akhenaten and Nefertiti's third daughter Ankhesenpaaten may also have been married to her father, as there is evidence of another princess born late in his reign called Ankhesenpaaten Tasherit. However, the picture is confused by the fact that both Meretaten and Ankhesenpaaten were later married to young men who were heirs to the Egyptian throne.

## DUAL RULING

The period just before the death of Akhenaten in 1336 BCE is a confusing time for modern scholars. Many facts and personalities are the subject of debate.

The problem is that there is actually little definite evidence from this period, and the few glimpses and pieces of information available seem to create as many problems as they resolve. In 1339 BCE, Akhenaten decided, like his father before him, to crown a co-regent who was called either Ankhkheperure Neferneferuaten or Ankhkheperure Smenkhkare. It is not known exactly who this person was or even if it was actually two different people. It may have been a fourteen-year-old son of Akhenaten and Kiya called Smenkhkare, who was married to the princess Meretaten, or it may have been someone else completely.

An area of particular uncertainty today is the fate of Nefertiti. She seems to disappear from view in 1341 BCE, and it is possible that this is when she died. However, another theory is that Nefertiti didn't die but changed her name to Ankhkheperure Neferneferuaten and became co-ruler with her husband. Some scholars also think that after the death of Akhenaten she changed her name yet again and became the sole pharaoh called Ankh-kheperure Smenkhkare. This would mean that the man Smenkhkare did not exist, and the marriage to Meretaten was symbolic only. The solution to this question may lie with the mummy of a young man that was found in Tomb 55 in the Valley of the Kings at Thebes. Many think this is the body of Smenkhkare, which would mean that the co-regent and pharaoh Smenkhkare couldn't have been Nefertiti in disguise. However, other scholars dispute this view and believe that the mummy may be that of Akhenaten or even someone else.

## AKHENATEN'S LAST DAYS

We know little about Akhenaten's final years, although images of him suggest that he put on quite a lot of weight. Akhenaten died in the seventeenth year of his rule, 1336 BCE. Unfortunately, his tomb in the eastern cliffs wasn't finished. The original tomb plan was hurriedly changed and a pillared corridor was converted into the burial chamber. The floor of this room was lowered so the king's limestone sarcophagus would fit, and the walls were plastered and decorated. After the traditional seventy days taken to embalm his mummy, the pharaoh Akhenaten was buried in the tomb overlooking his new capital city of Akhetaten. With the death of Akhenaten the great champion of the religion of the god Aten had gone. It is apparent that people had already been growing tired of the new religion, based so firmly on the king and his family. Subversive cartoons have been found that show the king and queen as monkeys, and small statues of traditional gods were increasingly appearing in peoples' homes. Immediately after Akhenaten's death, the traditional gods of Egypt were included in religious ceremonies once more.

## THE SUCCESSION OF TUTANKHAMEN

One cannot be sure how long the next pharaoh, Ankhkheperure Smenkhkare, ruled Egypt, but it was probably for less than a year. He was succeeded by a nine-year-old boy called Tutankhaten, who was probably the younger son of Akhenaten and Kiya, as there is one inscribed block from the city of Akhetaten that describes him as "the king's bodily son, his beloved,

This image likely shows what Tutankhaten looked like. He was made pharaoh when he was only nine years old.

Tutankhaten." Tutankhaten was married to Akhenaten and Nefertiti's third daughter, Ankhesenpaaten, who was about fourteen years old at the time.

Tutankhaten seems to have been heavily influenced by his great uncle Ay, the man who was the brother of Queen Tiye and who may have been the father of Nefertiti. Ay had led a successful career during the reign of Akhenaten, and he had moved with the royal court to Akhetaten. A large tomb had been prepared for him at the Southern Tombs, with an important religious document called "The Great Hymn to Aten," probably written by Akhenaten, inscribed on its walls. Ay had risen to the position of vizier in the government and was probably one of Akhenaten's closest advisers.

## TUTANKHATEN'S CHANGES

One cannot tell whether the changes made in the next few years were Tutankhaten's or Ay's idea, but it is probable that the old, seasoned politician was the driving force. Building work was soon resumed on the new temples at Thebes, which had been left unfinished with Akhenaten's move to Akhetaten. In the second year of Tutankhaten's reign, when he was just eleven years old, he and his wife Ankhesenpaaten decided to change their names, signaling an end to the dominance of the god Aten. Tutankhaten became Tutankhamen, and Ankhesenpaaten became Ankhesenamen.

At the beginning of Tutankhamen's third year of rule, 1334 BCE, the royal family and the government left the city of Akhetaten and moved to the old capital city at Memphis. Although some poorer people seem to have stayed behind in their new homes at Akhetaten, most of the inhabitants of the palaces and villas also abandoned the city as the professional classes followed the court back to Memphis. All the furnishings of these houses were carefully packed up and shipped out, and doors and windows were carefully bricked up. Many things no longer required were left behind, which is very lucky for modern archaeologists, who have been able to dig up all the unwanted objects. These include the "files" from the "Place of the Letters of Pharaoh" and many beautiful models of the heads of Akhenaten, Nefertiti, Kiya, and the royal daughters from the workshops of the sculptor Thutmose.

Work also stopped on the Northern and Southern Tombs, and the occupants of the work-

# KING TUT'S TOMB

Preparations began on a tomb for the new pharaoh in the Valley of the Kings at Thebes. Tutankhamen was eventually buried in a small tomb that may either have been adapted from an already existing unfinished

Archaeologist Howard Carter made one of the greatest discoveries of the twentieth century when he uncovered Tutankhamen's tomb. Unfortunately, it was soon robbed.

tomb or may have been abruptly finished because of his sudden, unexpected death at about the age of eighteen. Although robbed soon after burial, the entrance and location of his tomb were quickly covered up with heaps of rubble and forgotten. On November 4, 1922, archaeologist Howard Carter uncovered the first step of the staircase leading down to the entrance of Tutankhamen's tomb. Carter's subsequent finds inside the tomb of an almost complete Eighteenth Dynasty royal burial are staggering in their richness, and it is still famous today as one of the most important archaeological discoveries of the twentieth century.

ers' village returned to their homes in another village known as Deir el-Medina on the west bank at Thebes. Every single tomb at el-Amarna was left unfinished and, with the exception of Akhenaten's tomb, it is unlikely that they were ever used.

Once back at the old capital Memphis, Tutankhamen focused on renovating and reopening temples to all the major gods in Egypt. A large stele was erected in the temple at Karnak that explained his wishes. "When his Person appeared as king, the temples and cities of gods and goddesses, from Elephantine [Aswan] as far as the Delta marshes, were fallen into decay and their shrines were fallen into ruin, having become mere mounds overgrown with grass. And his person made monuments for the gods, making their statues out of the best gold from foreign lands, building their shrines anew as monuments endowed with possessions forever."

Although Tutankhamen was probably exaggerating about the poor condition of the temples, it certainly was true that many cult statues of Amen in particular had been destroyed during the reign of Akhenaten. These statues were the focal point of each temple, as they were thought to be inhabited by the gods during religious services. By ordering the replacement of these images, Tutankhamen was not only giving back to the temples their most important objects, but he was also signaling that the pharaoh and his closest advisers believed once more in the other gods of Egypt. Most of the statues Tutankhamen commissioned were given the facial features of the new pharaoh and many are recognizable today.

Many new priests were also appointed, including teams for the great Amen temples at Thebes.

"He [Tutankhamen] installed ordinary priests and higher clergy from among the children of the officials of their cities, each one the son of a notable person." New administrators were also appointed to look after the financial affairs of each temple and to ensure the supply of offerings to the gods. Tutankhamen also seems to have rejected the ideas that Akhenaten had about how the pharaoh should be presented. There were no more images of the pharaoh and his family lounging about. More traditional pictures appeared of the pharaoh hunting in his chariot and smiting his enemies over the head.

Tutankhamen died unexpectedly at the young age of only eighteen years, leaving behind a wild tangle of theories surrounding his abrupt departure, including death as a result of a hunting injury and even assassination. More likely, the young ruler died of complications from a mosquito-borne illness known as malaria, or he may have had an unusual bone disease. His short stint as ruler may be marked by his tomb containing three perhaps ostentatious coffins, but while he was on the throne he did kick-start much-needed construction within Egypt as well as restore the country's traditional religion.

**Benben stone** A short cone-shaped stone that was placed in total sunlight for sun rituals; sacred to the Egyptian god Ra.

**cartouche** Symbols enclosed by a border design, a kind of royal stamp.

**coronation** The rituals, including feasts, ceremonies, and rites, by which Egyptian pharaohs were made rulers and formally given their power.

**cult** Groups of people who express devotion or veneration toward a particular deity or holy location or object.

**democratize** To make something more open and accessible to people.

**dynasty** Egyptian history was divided into thirty-one dynasties stretching from Menes in the First Dynasty until the invasion of Alexander the Great in 332 BCE. The reason for the change from one dynasty to the next is not always clear, but is usually connected to a change in the royal family or the location of the capital.

**Froehlich's syndrome** A syndrome usually acquired by males with characteristics including delayed puberty and obesity; caused by pituitary gland abnormalities.

**harvest or shemu** The season between April and June when crops were harvested.

**Heb Sed festival** The ritual of royal regeneration, usually celebrated after thirty years of the king's reign but occasionally performed earlier.

**henotheistic** The characteristic of believing in and

worshipping one god while accepting the possibility that other gods might exist.

**Lower Egypt** The northern half of the country stretching from Memphis to the Mediterranean coast.

**Maat** A goddess who embodied aspects of truth, justice, and harmony in the universe. The power of Maat regulated the seasons and the movement of the sun, the moon, and the stars. One of the main jobs of the king was to maintain the rule of Maat.

**Marfan's syndrome** A disease characterized by extremely long, skinny fingers, as well as visual and cardiovascular issues.

**Memphis** Capital city of Ancient Egypt, close to modern-day Cairo. The city was the cult center of the god Ptah.

**Nubia** The region immediately south of ancient Egypt (modern-day Sudan).

**pharaoh** From the New Kingdom onward the term pharaoh was used for the ruler of Egypt.

**sarcophagus** A coffin made from stone and often decorated, often found in ancient Egypt, Greece, and Rome.

**Sekhmet** A goddess in the form of a lioness who was viewed as the bringer of slaughter and pestilence as well as a fierce protector.

**stele or stela** A stone column or slab that sits upright, usually with a religious design and sometimes used as a gravestone.

**Upper Egypt** The southern half of the country stretching from Memphis to Aswan.

**Valley of the Kings** New Kingdom royal necropolis located on the west bank of the Nile, about 3 miles west of modern Luxor.

**vizier** The vizier or tjaty was the chief minister of the government. During the New Kingdom there were two viziers, one at Memphis and one at Thebes.

American Research Center in Egypt (U.S. Office)
8700 Crownhill Blvd., Suite 507
San Antonio, TX 78209-1130
(210) 821-7000
E-mail: info@arce.org
Website: http://www.arce.org
The American Research Center in Egypt (ARCE) supports education, training, and preservation of Egypt and its cultural heritage.

*Ancient Egypt Magazine*
1 Newton Street
Manchester M1 1HW
England
E-mail: empire@globalnet.co.uk
Website: http://www.ancientegyptmagazine.co.uk
*Ancient Egypt Magazine* is a collection of articles written by Egyptology experts about news, research, findings, excavations and more for an audience of both Egyptology professionals as well as those who are interested in ancient Egypt.

Archaeological Institute of America Headquarters
Boston University
656 Beacon Street, 6th Floor
Boston, MA 02215-2006
E-mail: aia@aia.bu.edu
Website: https://www.archaeological.org
The Archaeological Institute of America (AIA) is the oldest and largest group in North America that dedicates itself to all things archaeology.

California Classical Association—Northern Section
Attn: Gillian McIntosh, Treasurer
581 Frederick Street
San Francisco, CA 94117
Website: http://www.ccanorth.org/
The CCA encourages the instruction and training of Classics such as through conferences and relationships with other classical organizations.

The Classical Association of Canada
Department of Greek and Roman Studies
University of Victoria
Victoria, BC V8W 3P4
Canada
(250) 721-8528
Website: http://cac-scec.ca
This nonprofit organization was formed in 1947 to promote the study of Greek and Roman civilizations as well as how they affected later societies and modern culture.

## WEBSITES

Because of the changing nature of internet links, Rosen Publishing has developed an online list of websites related to the subject of this book. This site is updated regularly. Please use this link to access the list:

http://www.rosenlinks.com/LANW/tutank

Aldred, Cyril. *Akhenaten, King of Egypt*. London, UK, and New York, NY: Thames & Hudson, 2001.

Aldred, Cyril, and Aidan Dodson. *The Egyptians*, 3rd edition. London, UK, and New York, NY: Thames & Hudson, 2005.

Amstutz, Lisa J. *Ancient Egypt* (Ancient Civilizations). North Mankato, MN: ABDO Publishing, 2015.

Baines, John, and Jaromir Malek. *Atlas of Ancient Egypt*, Rev. edition. New York, NY: Facts on File, 2005.

Baker, Rosalie F. *Ancient Egyptians: People of the Pyramids*. New York, NY: Oxford University Press, 2001.

Fletcher, Joann. *Chronicle of a Pharaoh: The Intimate Life of Amenhotep III*. New York, NY: Oxford University Press, 2002.

Hollar, Sherman. *Ancient Egypt*. New York, NY: Britannica Educational Publishing, 2012.

Kuiper, Kathleen. *Ancient Egypt*. New York, NY: Britannica Educational Publishing, 2011.

Lange, Brenda. *Nefertiti* (Ancient World Leaders). New York, NY: Chelsea House, 2013. Ebook.

Reeves, Nicholas. *Akhenaten, Egypt's False Prophet*. London, UK, and New York, NY: Thames & Hudson, 2005.

Reeves, Nicholas. *The Complete Tutankhamun: The King, the Tomb, the Royal Treasure*. London, UK, and New York, NY: Thames & Hudson, 2007.

Shaw, Ian, and Paul Nicholson. *British Museum Dictionary of Ancient Egypt*. Princeton, NJ: Princeton University Press, 2008.

Shea, Therese. *Discovering Egyptian Dynasties* (Exploring African Civilizations). New York, NY: Rosen Publishing, 2014.

Staley, Erin. *Discovering Ancient Egypt*. New York, NY: Britannica Educational Publishing, 2015.

"Akhenaten (reigned 1352–1336 BC)." BBC. 2014. Retrieved May 23, 2016 (http://www.bbc.co.uk/history/historic_figures/akhenaten.shtml).

Arnold, Dorothea. *The Royal Women of Amarna.* New York, NY: Metropolitan Museum of Art, 1996.

BBC. "Witness, Tomb of Tutankhamun." November 30, 2010. Retrieved May 26, 2016 (http://www.bbc.co.uk/programmes/p00c5ww8).

Breasted, James. *Ancient Records of Egypt Vol II: The Eighteenth Dynasty*. Urbana, IL: University of Illinois Press, 2001.

Davies, Norman de Garis. *The Rock Tombs of El Amarna.* (Parts I to VI). London, UK: Egypt Exploration Society, 1903–1908.

Dunn, Jimmy. "Egypt: Tutankhamun (King Tut) of the 18th Dynasty—King Tut." Tour Egypt. August 21, 2011. Retrieved May 26, 2016 (http://www.touregypt.net/featurestories/tut.htm).

"Egypt: Rulers, Kings and Pharaohs of Ancient Egypt: Amenhotep IV (Akhenaten)." Tour Egypt. April 26, 2011. Retrieved May 23, 2016 (http://www.touregypt.net/18dyn10.htm).

Hornung, Erik. *Akhenaten and the Religion of Light*. Ithaca,

NY: Cornell University Press, 1999.

Kemp, Barry. *Ancient Egypt: Anatomy of a Civilization.* London, UK, and New York, NY: Routledge, 1989.

Lichtheim, Miriam. *Ancient Egyptian Literature Volume II: The New Kingdom.* Berkeley, CA: University of California Press, 1976.

Moran, William. *The Amarna Letters.* Baltimore, MD: John Hopkins University Press, 1992.

Murnane, William. *Texts from the Amarna Period in Egypt.* Atlanta, GA: Scholars Press, 1995.

Spence, Kate. "Akhenaten and the Amarna Period." BBC. February 17, 2011. Retrieved May 23, 2016 (www.bbc.co.uk/history/ancient/egyptians/akhenaten_01.shtml).

"The Talatat Wall, an Amarna Jigsaw Puzzle." The Amarna Site. 1997. Retrieved June 20, 2016 (http://www.amarna.co.uk/talatat.php).

# ABOUT THE AUTHORS

Zoe Lowery is an avid student of history, constantly reading and getting lost in the fascinating stories like that of Akhenaten and Tutankhamen. She has edited a number of history books for Rosen Publishing and Enslow Publishing. She enjoys a quiet afternoon in just about any library, but especially those near her home in Colorado.

Susanna Thomas has a B.A. in Egyptian archaeology from University College, London, and was awarded a Ph.D. from Liverpool University in 2000. She has worked at sites all over Egypt, including the Valley of the Kings, and runs excavations at Tell Abqa'in in the western Delta. She has also been a research fellow at Liverpool University and director of the Ramesside Fortress Town Project. She is particularly interested in vitreous materials and trade in the late Bronze Age.

## PHOTO CREDITS

Cover, p. 3 (left) DEA/A. Dagli Orti/De Agostini/Getty Images; cover, p. 3 (right) Scott Olson/Getty Images; cover (background) Dudarev Mikhail/Shutterstock.com; pp. 7, 18, 24, 58, 76, 78–79 Werner Forman/Universal Images Group/Getty Images; p. 11 Wolfgang Kaehler/LightRocket/Getty Images; pp. 12–13 © City Image/Alamy Stock Photo; p. 14 zbg2/iStock/Thinkstock; p. 17 © Prisma Archivo/Alamy Stock Photo; pp. 30, 54–55, 66 Print Collector/Hulton Archive/Getty Images; pp. 32–33, 61 Universal Images Group/Getty Images; pp. 38–39 DEA/G. Sioen/De Agostini/Getty Images; p. 41 DEA/ S. Vannini/De Agostini/Getty Images; pp. 50–51, 74 © Jim Henderson/Alamy Stock Photo; pp. 62–63 PHAS/Universal Images Group/Getty Images; p. 65 Science & Society Picture Library/Getty Images; pp. 70–71, 82–83 Universal History Archive/Universal Images Group/Getty Images; pp. 84–85 DEA/G. Dagli Orti/De Agostini/Getty Images; p. 93 AFP/Getty Images; pp. 96–97 Time Life Pictures/The LIFE Picture Collection/Getty Images; interior pages background images © iStockphoto.com/kikkalek5050 (sky), Triff/Shutterstock.com (map).

Designer: Brian Garvey; Editor: Heather Moore Niver; Photo Researcher: Heather Moore Niver